My Friend the Witch: Kara-Madjo

Nadia Ahidjo

To my daughters, may your lives always be as vivid as your imagination

My name is Sahra. I love Halloween, witches, and all things scary! That is why this morning, when I woke up, I decided to become friends with a witch. I think it would be fun! We could learn lots of spells, and we could even go to school together and scare my friends.

With that in mind, I went into the kitchen of our little house, made a little snack, and put it in my bag. I also packed a small umbrella, a small hat, and boots in case it rained... and I went into the forest for a walk and to look for a witch, who would like to be my friend.

While walking, I met many small birds and other animals which can only be found in a forest. I said to all of them - "Hello, do you know where I can find the witch?" They all replied, "yes, follow the path lined with red flowers, and at the end, you will find, the witch Kara-Madjo's house."

I went along that path, and finally came to a clearing, where there was a little yellow house with red shutters and tiny spiders hanging from the roof. I knocked on the door and shouted loudly, "hello my name is Sahra. I have come to visit you and become your friend!"

The door suddenly opened, and there appeared on the doorstep, a little lady, with purple hair. She said to me, with a big smile "Oooooooh" that's so kind, please come in, come in, welcome my friend.

"Do you know that you are the first person who has come to my house to be my friend?" Everyone I try to talk to screams in fear. They do not even try to listen to me or to find out whether I am nice or not. They just think I'm a witch, and they run away."

I was surprised to hear that, because the witch's house smelled so good, she had baked an apple pie. She invited me into her kitchen, cut me a big piece, and we had a snack together. We had lots of fun all afternoon.

At the end of the day, my friend, Kara-Madjo, invited me to come back the next day so that she could share the recipe for her apple pie with me.

I came home happy to have made a new friend, and was in a hurry to tell Mom about my day. I was surprised when Mom told me, "You know, I know Kara-Madjo too. But what you don't know, is that she has two names because she can be nice one day, and not so nice another day. When she is nice we call her Kara, and when she is not so nice, we call her Madjo. You just have to make sure that you visit her on the right day!"

I was a little confused by all this. "But Mom, how would I know if it is a good day or if it is a bad day? Mom gave me a tip, she told me that on days when she is nice, she always bakes apple pies... but when she is not, she drinks lots of coffee. "So, my little Sahra, as soon as you enter her house, the smell will tell you if it is a good day or a bad day for your friend the witch."

I thanked Mom, and went to bed excited thinking about the next day. The next day, I packed my bag again and went back to my friend, Kara-Madjo's house.

But the person who opened the door had a face so upset that I started to wonder if it was a good day for my friend, the witch.

"Who is here, little girl?" What do you want?

"She didn't even recognise me anymore, it made me very sad". But it's me Kara-Madjo, I was here yesterday, don't you remember me? She still let me in though, slamming the door shut, and that's when I smelled coffee all over the house.

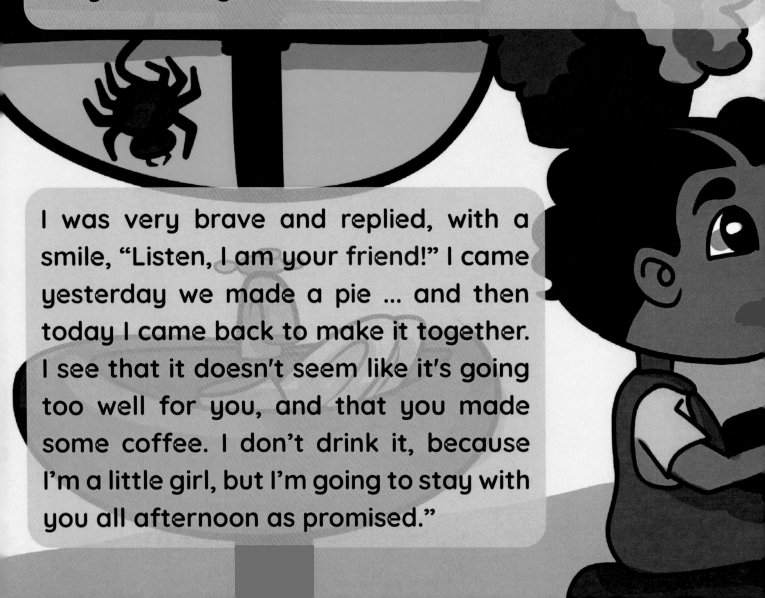

That's when I realized that it was not the best day for my friend the witch. I followed her into her kitchen anyway, and sat down at the table with her. She suddenly looked at me, without a smile, and grumblingly, asked "So what are you looking for here?"

I was very brave and replied, with a smile, "Listen, I am your friend!" I came yesterday we made a pie … and then today I came back to make it together. I see that it doesn't seem like it's going too well for you, and that you made some coffee. I don't drink it, because I'm a little girl, but I'm going to stay with you all afternoon as promised."

Kara-Madjo was amazed, she looked at me surprised. "But, little girl aren't you afraid of me? You want to stay here with me even though I'm not in a good mood? Aren't you afraid that I will eat you, or worse put a spell on you?"

"No Kara-Madjo, whether you're having a good day or a bad day, I will always be your friend!" I spent the whole day with my friend the witch, and although we did not have much fun because she was not having a good day, I stayed with her anyway.

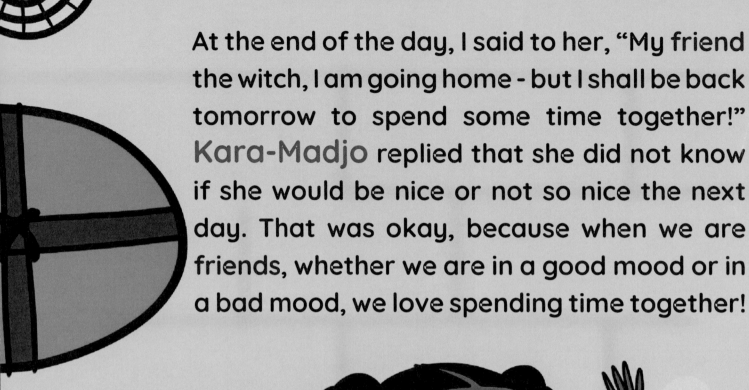

At the end of the day, I said to her, "My friend the witch, I am going home - but I shall be back tomorrow to spend some time together!" Kara-Madjo replied that she did not know if she would be nice or not so nice the next day. That was okay, because when we are friends, whether we are in a good mood or in a bad mood, we love spending time together!

"Goodbye Kara-Madjo, see you tomorrow!"

The End

Made in United States
North Haven, CT
14 January 2022

14769883R00018